Team Stats—Football Edition

HIGHLIGHTS OF THE KANSAS CITY CHIEFS

MARYSA STORM

BLACK RABBIT BOOKS

Bolt is published by Black Rabbit Books
P.O. Box 3263, Mankato, Minnesota, 56002.
www.blackrabbitbooks.com

Jennifer Besel, editor; Michael Sellner, interior designer; Grant Gould, cover designer; Omay Ayres, photo researcher

Cataloging-in-Publication Data is available at the Library of Congress.
ISBN 978-1-68072-887-3 (library binding)
ISBN 978-1-68072-893-4 (e-book)
ISBN 978-1-64466-084-3 (paperback)

Printed in the United States of America. 1/19

Image Credits

AP Images: AP, 4–5; Ben Margot, 26; DICK WHIPPLE, 16–17 (Holmes); G. Newman Lowrance, 1; Kevin Terrell, 14; LIEBB, 23; Ric Tapia, 3, 16–17 (bkgd); commons.wikimedia.org: 10–11 (trophey); Getty: Brian Bahr, 22; Focus on Sport, 8–9, 10, 18–19; Jed Jacobsohn /Allsport, 20 (b); Jonathan Daniel, 25; Newscom: Peter Aiken, 20 (t); Scott Winters/Icon Sportswire, 28–29 (t); Shutterstock: enterlinedesign, 28–29 (b); Orgus88, 24; Svyatoslav Aleksandrov, 31; VitaminCo, 8 (ball), 19, 32; tshaonline.org: TSHA, 6; tumblr.com: TicoBaul, 12–13; USA Today Sports: Kevin Jairaj, Cover

Every effort has been made to contact copyright holders for material reproduced in this book. Any omissions will be rectified in subsequent printings if notice is given to the publisher.

CONTENTS

CHAPTER 1

On the FIELD

In 1970, the Kansas City Chiefs played the AFL Championship game. Its **opponents**, the Oakland Raiders, had beat it twice that season. The Chiefs were determined to win this time.

At halftime, the game was tied. But the Chiefs refused to let the Raiders win. In the third quarter, the Chiefs **intercepted** the ball. Then came a touchdown! The Chiefs won!

CHAPTER 2

HISTORY of the Chiefs

The Chiefs began playing in 1960. At the time, it played in Dallas as the Texans. The Dallas Cowboys had also formed that year, though. The city couldn't support both teams. In 1963, the Texans moved to Kansas City. The team became the Chiefs.

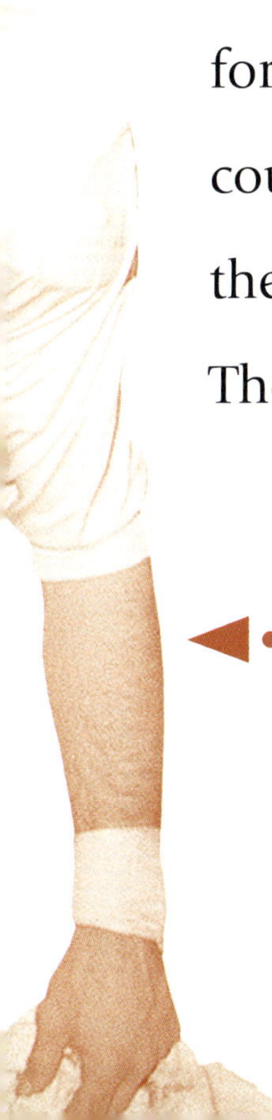

Successful Seasons

As both the Texans and Chiefs, the team was successful. Head coach Hank Stram led it to many wins. In fact, the team played the first ever Super Bowl in 1967. It lost that game. But the team won the big game in 1970.

In 1971, the Chiefs played the NFL's longest game. The game went into two overtimes. Overtime lasted 22 minutes and 40 seconds.

CHAPTER 3

Greatest MOMENTS

The Chiefs' history is full of big games. Fans love to look back on these moments.

Few people thought the Chiefs would win the 1970 Super Bowl. Its opponents, the Minnesota Vikings, ranked as one of the best teams. The Chiefs crushed the Vikings. Its **defense** only allowed the Vikings 239 yards. And its **offense** just kept scoring. The Chiefs won 23–7.

Making a Record

During a 1990 game, linebacker Derrick Thomas was nearly unstoppable. He kept taking down the Seattle Seahawks' quarterback. Thomas made seven **sacks**. No one had made that many sacks in a game before.

Winning a Playoff Game

In 2016, the Chiefs played the Houston Texans in the AFC Wild Card game. The Chiefs dominated. The team scored immediately after the game began. And the players didn't stop. They made 30 total points. The Texans couldn't score once. This big win meant a lot. It was the Chiefs' first **playoff** win in 22 seasons.

BY THE NUMBERS

(as of 2018)

916

team record for most career receptions
(Tony Gonzalez)

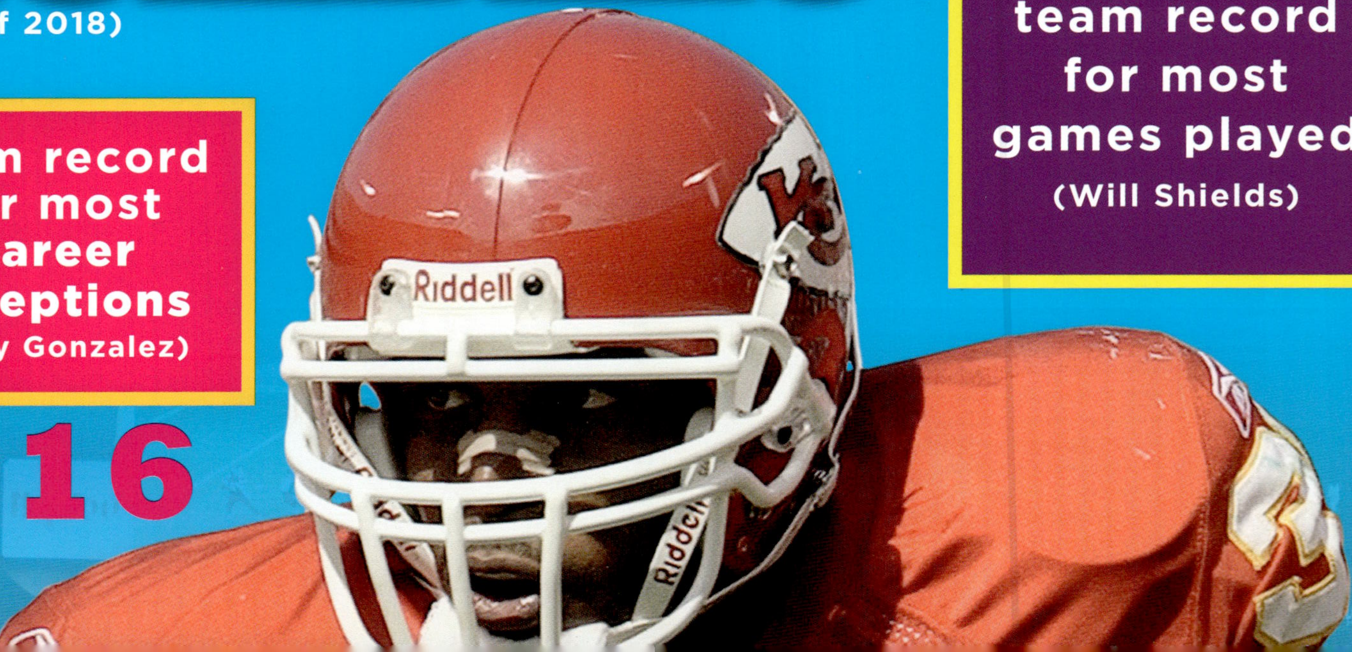

224

team record for most games played
(Will Shields)

10
total retired jersey numbers

76
team record for most career rushing touchdowns
(Priest Holmes)

CHAPTER 4

STARS of the Chiefs

The Chiefs' greatest moments wouldn't have been possible without amazing players.

Quarterback Len Dawson led the Chiefs to many victories. He helped the team win the 1970 Super Bowl. He made many team records.

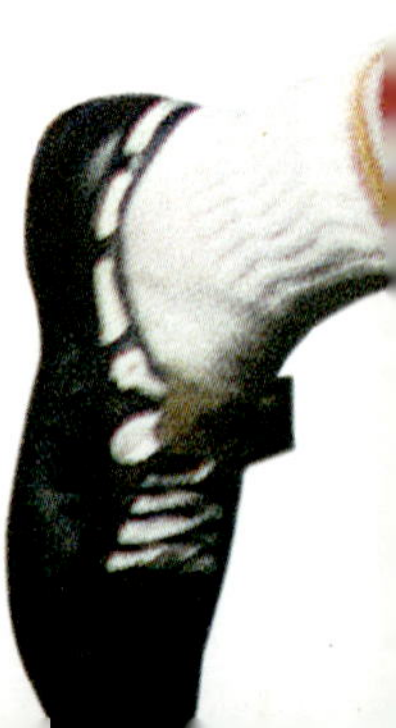

Dawson's TEAM Records

most passes attempted
3,696

most pass completions
2,115

most passing yards
28,507

most touchdown passes
237

Tony Gonzalez

Tony Gonzalez was an amazing tight end. He was tough to block. He holds tight-end records for most receptions and receiving yards. Many people call him the NFL's greatest tight end.

Gonzalez played college basketball before pro football.

Will Shields

Will Shields played guard for the Chiefs. He went to the Pro Bowl 12 times in a row. Shields was dedicated. He never missed a game.

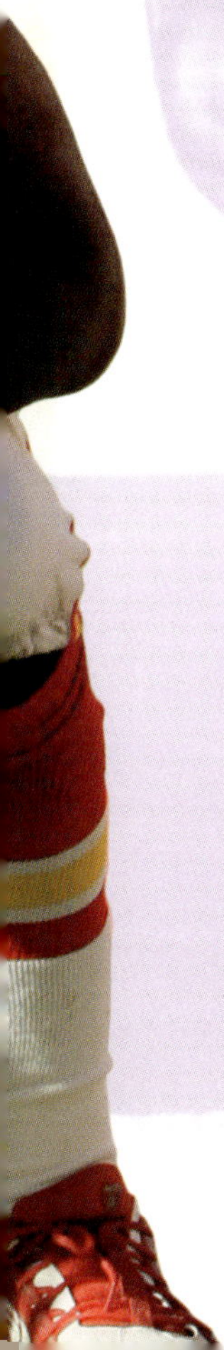

Willie Lanier

The Chiefs drafted Willie Lanier in 1967. He became the first African American to star as middle linebacker. Lanier was a smart player and was hard to block.

Derrick Thomas

Derrick Thomas also played linebacker. Thomas was a beast on the field. He made 126.5 sacks during his 11-season career. As of 2018, his record for most sacks in one game hasn't been broken.

Priest Holmes

Priest Holmes was a star running back. He raced down the field to make incredible touchdowns. Holmes had the most yards in 2002 and 2003. In 2003, he made a record 27 touchdowns in one season.

Over the years, the Chiefs has had many amazing moments. Fans can't wait to see what it does next.

Holmes' touchdown record was broken in 2005.

TIMELINE

1955

1960
Team starts playing.

1962
Dawson joins team.

1963
Team moves to Kansas City.

1970
Team wins its first Super Bowl.

1989
Thomas joins team.

1997
Chiefs draft Gonzalez.

2016
Team wins first playoff game in 22 seasons.

2019
Team plays first AFL Championship game since 1993.

2020

GLOSSARY

career (kuh-REER)—a period of time spent in a job

defense (DEE-fens)—the players on a team who try to stop the other team from scoring

intercept (in-tur-SEPT)—to catch a pass made by the other team

offense (AW-fens)—the group of players in control of the ball trying to score points

opponent (uh-POH-nunt)—a person, team, or group that is competing against another

playoff (PLAY-ahf)—a series of games played after the regular season to decide which player or team is the champion

reception (ree-SEP-shun)—catching a pass thrown toward the opponent's goal

rushing (RUSH-ing)—moving the football toward the goal using running plays

sack (SAK)—a tackle of the quarterback before he or she crosses the line of scrimmage

LEARN MORE

BOOKS

Burgess, Zack. *Meet the Kansas City Chiefs.* Big Picture Sports. Chicago: Norwood House Press, 2017.

Clausen-Grace, Nicki, and Jeff Grace. *Football Science.* Got Game. Mankato, MN: Black Rabbit Books, 2018.

Morey, Allan. *The Kansas City Chiefs Story.* NFL Teams. Minneapolis: Bellwether Media, Inc., 2017.

WEBSITES

Football: National Football League
www.ducksters.com/sports/national_football_league.php

Kansas City Chiefs Team Page
www.nfl.com/teams/kansascitychiefs/profile?team=KC

Official Website of the Kansas City Chiefs
www.chiefs.com

INDEX